Violet
Mackerel's
Personal Space

Essex

D1589465

3013020321603 8

Other stories about Violet Mackerel:

Violet Mackerel's Personal Space

ANNA BRANFORD

illustrated by
SAM WILSON

WALKER
BOOKS

First published 2012 by Walker Books Australia Pty Ltd

First published in the UK 2013 by Walker Books Ltd
87 Vauxhall Walk, London SE11 5HJ

2 4 6 8 10 9 7 5 3 1

Text © 2013 Anna Branford
Illustrations © 2013 Sam Wilson

This book has been typeset in Bembo

Printed and bound in Great Britain by Clays Ltd, St Ives plc

British Library Cataloguing in Publication Data:
a catalogue record for this book is available from the British Library

ISBN 978-1-4063-2696-3

www.walker.co.uk

www.violetmackerel.com

For Kate (my sister)
AB

For my children George and Molly
SW

The
Pink Shell

Violet Mackerel is on a summer holiday at the beach with her sister, Nicola, her brother, Dylan, her mum and her mum's boyfriend, Vincent.

It is nearly the end of the holiday and Violet is wishing it was still the beginning.

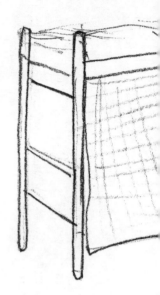

At the beach house where they have been staying there are bunk beds. Violet has been sleeping on the bottom bunk. She has tucked a sheet under the mattress of the top bunk and dangled it down, so it is a small **personal space** of her own. You can't do that with an ordinary bed like the one at Violet's normal house. It has to be a bunk bed.

It has been quite a good holiday. Violet likes Vincent making pancakes

 for everyone each morning. She likes going for walks to look in rock pools and having the sound of the sea in her ears all the time. She likes it after dinner when they roll up their trousers for an evening paddle and their trousers get wet anyway and no one minds. And since no one has to get up at any particular time, no one has to go to bed at any particular time either, so they sit up late on the verandah, chatting and burning citronella candles to keep the mosquitoes away.

On the last
morning of
the holiday,
everyone puts all
their things back in their
suitcases. Violet takes the sheet down
from the bunk bed and folds it up. One
minute it looks as if her family actually
does live in the beach house, and the
next minute it looks as if they have
never stayed there at all.

Mum says, "Before we go, let's all
have one final check and make sure
we haven't left anything behind."
So everyone has a look behind the
couch and in the little cupboard in
the bathroom and under the coffee

table. Violet thinks she might pull up the corner of her mattress and have a look under that. There is a row of flat wooden slats with little spaces between them. And in one of the spaces there is a small pink shell.

It isn't one of Violet's shells. She has collected lots of shells but they are packed carefully in a box in her suitcase with the pieces of tumbled glass she found on the beach. This pink shell has been left there by someone else.

Violet wonders who it could have been. Maybe it was someone else who slept on the bottom bunk and didn't want to go home. Maybe they left the small pink shell behind on purpose.

This thought gives Violet a good idea for a new **theory**, the

Theory of Leaving

Small
Things Behind.

The **theory** is this: maybe wherever you leave something small, a tiny part of you gets to stay too.

Violet opens her suitcase, finds her box and takes out a little piece of green tumbled glass. She presses it into the space beside the pink shell and covers it all up again, smoothing the mattress. No one sees.

"Finished," calls Violet, going to join the others. She puts her suitcase in the boot of the car next to Mum's.

Before they leave, she has one last look at the room. It looks exactly the same as it did before she stayed there. But it is not. Somehow, this idea makes Violet feel a bit less sad about the summer holiday being finished.

It is a long drive from the beach back to her house, so she has lots of time to think about her new theory and about all the places she might like to leave **small things**. She would like to hide a sequin up the Eiffel Tower,

and bury a little glass bead somewhere
in the African wilderness, and slip a

silver star under
a stone in an old
English castle.

It would be like
a little trail of
Violet all through
the world.

The Picnic Dinner

At home that evening, dinner is a funny mix of things which were in the kitchen before the holiday and are still OK to eat, like baked beans and corn chips and dried pawpaw spears, which Violet quite likes.

But even though it is more like a picnic than actual dinner, Mum has put proper wine glasses on the table for everyone and Vincent is filling them up with pink lemonade.

When everyone is sitting down, Vincent puts his arm around Mum and says, "We have some special news."

Violet nibbles a pawpaw spear and hopes the news will be about getting a kitten.

"Vincent and I have decided we would like to get married," says Mum.

A funny feeling comes into the kitchen and no one says anything.

Violet wants to say something, but it is hard to think of what. Last year her teacher, Miss Wuthering, got married and came back from her holiday being called Mrs Chan. She showed Violet's class a picture of herself in a long white dress with sparkles in her hair.

"Will you change your name and put sparkles in your hair?" asks Violet.

"Well," says Mum, "I'll still be a Mackerel, but I might put sparkles in my hair."

Vincent says, "We were thinking we might have a small wedding in the garden and just invite a few special guests."

"Can I make
paper cranes for
the guests?" asks
Nicola.

"We'd love that,"
says Vincent.

"Can I help you make
a wedding dress?"
asks Violet.

"Of course you can,"
says Mum.

Violet smiles
and Nicola is starting
to smile too. Violet
thinks Mum will
look lovely with
sparkles in her hair.

18

"But there isn't room in our house for any more people," says Dylan, who is not smiling. "We already hardly fit."

It is true that it's already sometimes a bit squishy with Mum, Nicola, Dylan and Violet, especially when they all need to go to the bathroom at exactly the same time.

"Well, that's the other part of the news," says Mum. "We'll have to move to a slightly bigger place if we're all going to live together. We're going to need to find a new home soon, in fact."

"No," says Dylan. "I'm not moving anywhere."

Then he goes upstairs and slams his bedroom door shut.

After that, the picnic dinner doesn't seem quite so nice.

The Shuffling Noise

Violet would like to
knock on Dylan's door
and see if he wants some
pink lemonade or corn
chips (she has eaten all
the pawpaw spears) but
Mum says Dylan's room
is his **personal space**

and when he's inside it with the door closed, that means he probably just wants to be by himself for a while. So after dinner Violet goes up to her room and writes a small note with a pencil. It says:

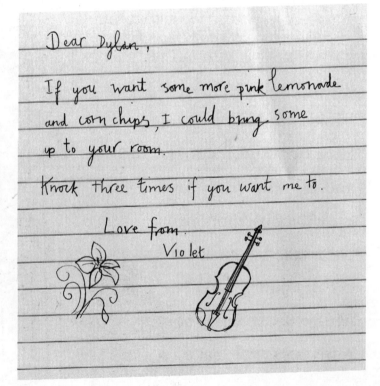

Dear Dylan,

If you want some more pink lemonade and corn chips, I could bring some up to your room.

Knock three times if you want me to.

Love from
Violet

At the end of the note she draws a small violin, because Dylan is a very good violin player, and a small violet, because that is her name. She slides the note under Dylan's door and waits to see if there is any knocking, but there is none − just a strange shuffling and rummaging of things being moved around.

Later on, after Vincent has gone home, Mum chats with Nicola in her bedroom. Violet is still waiting outside Dylan's door in case there is any knocking.

But there is only more shuffling and rummaging and soon Mum comes out of Nicola's room and says it is time for bed. She tucks Violet in.

"Is Nicola OK?" asks Violet.

"I think so," says Mum.

"Is Dylan OK?" asks Violet.

"Not just at the moment," says Mum. "I think it will probably take us all a while to figure everything out."

Violet is mostly quite good at figuring things out. Even though she doesn't remember Dad as well as the others because she was the youngest when he left, she knows that Dylan and Nicola both remember him well. And she knows that Dylan especially misses him very much.

"What about you?" Mum asks.
"Are you OK?"

Violet wonders whether or not she
is OK.

"Well, I am glad there is going to be
a wedding with sparkles in your hair
and paper cranes for the guests," says
Violet. "And I think it will be nice
if Vincent lives with us and makes

us pancakes
every day."
Mum
smiles.

"But I like us living here, even if it is a squish," says Violet. "And I don't like people being not OK by themselves in their rooms, even if it is their **personal space**."

"Neither do I," says Mum.

Then they have quite a long cuddle, because it is very tricky getting to sleep when there are people in your house who are not OK.

While she tries to sleep, Violet thinks about the tiny pink shell and the little piece of green tumbled glass hidden under the mattress at the beach house. If she closes her eyes it's almost as if she is there again, with the sheet dangling down and the soft noise of the sea in her ears. It is a nice thought. Much nicer than the thought of a newer, bigger house and much nicer than the thought of Dylan not being OK.

The **Theory of Leaving Small Things Behind** is quite a good **theory**, she thinks.

The Leaky Tent

Very early the next
morning the shuffling noise
in Dylan's room goes all
the way downstairs and
out into the back garden.
Sleepily, Violet goes over
to her window and
looks outside.

Dylan is putting up a tent that used to belong to Dad. Even though it is a bit leaky and musty, he keeps it in the back of his wardrobe and he even took it on his school camp last year. He said it was the worst tent of everyone in his class and he might as well have slept in a bin liner. But he still kept it.

First he lays the tent out on the ground and pins the floor down with L-shaped pegs. Then he slides long metal poles into the two seams at the front and back of the tent. And then he stretches out thin ropes from the two points of the tent and pegs them down into the ground too.

Violet thinks it looks a lot better than a bin liner. It looks even better than the bottom-bunk house she made with the sheet at the beach house. Violet thinks it is a very good tent.

Dylan unzips the front and starts putting things inside. He puts in his sleeping bag, a pillow, his chess set, his violin and a torch. And then he

goes inside and he doesn't come out.

Violet and Mum and Nicola have breakfast. It feels a bit funny without Dylan there. Mum is looking at the part of the newspaper where you can look for a new house. They will need to find one in just a couple of weeks, Mum says.

Violet wishes it didn't have to be so soon. She has never lived in another house except for the beach house and that was only for a few days. It is very hard to imagine living anywhere else and whenever she tries to think of it, she gets a funny feeling in her throat. She wonders if it's the same sort of feeling Dylan is having.

While Mum is in the shower and Nicola is getting dressed, Violet makes some toast and puts it on a tray with a note that says:

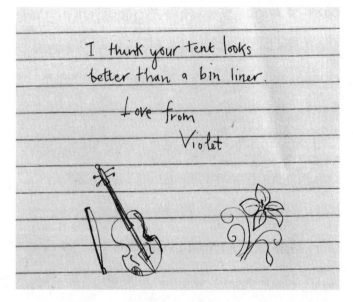

I think your tent looks
better than a bin liner.
Love from
Violet

She draws a violin and a violet again and then she goes outside and puts the tray just outside the zip-up door of Dylan's tent.

"There's some breakfast outside your front door," she shouts, since you can't knock on a tent.

There isn't any answer, just the slight rustling of a sleeping bag.

But when Violet goes up to her room and looks out the window, the tray has disappeared into the tent.

The House Hunt

Over the next few days, Mum and Vincent visit houses they read about in the newspaper. They visit a different one almost every morning because they need to find a house so soon. Sometimes Nicola and Violet go too.

Dylan mostly stays in his tent. So far, all the houses are either a bit too small, a bit too expensive, or a bit too far away.

Mum says things like, "But where would the dining table fit?" and Vincent says things like, "It might get a bit hot in the summer."

Violet doesn't mind so much about dining tables or hotness in the summer, but she does think that none of the houses look much like a proper home, where people could have dinner and do knitting and sort through boxes of **small things**. The new houses smell like paint and soap, not ginger cake or pumpkin soup. There isn't a web in any of the kitchen windows where a small friendly spider could live if he wanted to. And there isn't any music or chatting coming from any of the rooms. There is just the funny empty sound of no furniture.

But as well as house-hunting, there is lots of work to do to prepare for the small garden wedding, and Violet likes that much more.

Today, Vincent is building a special archway out of wire and bendy branches, big enough for him and Mum to walk under. It will be decorated with leaves and flowers for the wedding and Violet thinks it will look lovely in their garden, although

it might have to go a bit to the side
if Dylan is still living in his tent.

Mum is making a list of people to
invite and then crossing most of them
off again, since it will be such
a small wedding.

Nicola is folding paper
cranes and hanging them
on silver strings. They will
be gifts for the wedding guests
to take home. Violet watches her
sister's fingers folding and tweaking
and twiddling the little flat white
papers until they turn into perfect,
pointy birds. It is almost like magic,
Violet thinks. She hopes there will be
enough for her to have one too.

Violet is drawing pictures
of lovely wedding dresses
for Mum. Mum will be making
the dress with her sewing
machine, so she needs lots
of good ideas to help with
the design. Violet draws
long dresses and short dresses,
dresses with long trails, matching
hats, veils, jewels, flowers and
even one with fairy wings
and a wand, which Mum
says is actually her favourite,
but maybe not for a
wedding. In all of the
pictures, Violet draws
sparkles in Mum's hair.

At lunchtime, Violet takes a
sandwich, some juice and a banana
into the garden on a tray for Dylan.
She wonders if they will have to hire

a truck and move
Dylan's tent with
him still in it when
they finally do
find a new
house.

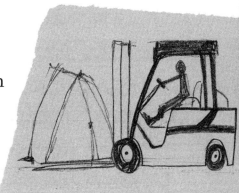

The Terrible Storm

Later in the afternoon there is a deep
rumbling in the sky.

"I heard on the radio that there was
going to be a storm," says Vincent,
who has finished working
on the wedding
archway and come
in for a cup of tea.

"What about Dylan?" asks Violet.

"Maybe he'll come inside," says Mum, hopefully.

Grey clouds are filling the sky and it is getting dark even though it's much too early for the sun to be going down. Violet goes outside.

"Dylan," she says. Then she waits. There is a little bit of rustling from inside the tent. "There's going to be a big storm tonight. Maybe you could come inside, just until it's over."

"No," says Dylan.

"What if your tent leaks?" asks Violet.

"I don't care," says Dylan.

"What if you have to sleep in a puddle?" asks Violet.

"I don't care," says Dylan, again.

There is already quite a strong wind blowing and Mum calls Violet back inside.

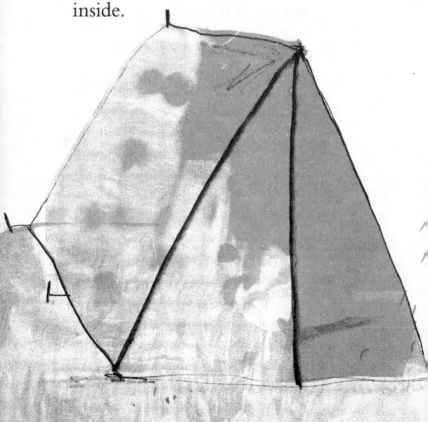

Normally, it is nice to be
inside the house with your
family when there is a big noisy storm
outside and there is pumpkin soup
for dinner and something on the TV
about penguins. But it is hard to enjoy
it when your brother is outside in the
garden in a leaky tent. Every now and
then the sky lights up outside and a
big crack of thunder makes everything
rattle. All of Violet's insides rattle too.

In every ad break, Violet and Mum
look out the window. Dylan's tent
looks more and more like one of
Nicola's paper cranes that didn't quite
work out and got crumpled and put in
the bin.

At the end of the penguin programme there is the clicking sound of the back door opening. Dylan stands in the doorway, shivering like one of the penguins in the documentary.

Violet has never seen anyone so wet, not even at the beach. There is water dripping from Dylan's nose and his ears. His pyjamas, which are completely stuck to him, make little rivers that run into a puddle all round his feet.

He is the bluish colour of a very cold person.

Mum runs over and hugs him. She doesn't even notice all the wetness and coldness getting on her. Water drips from the ends of Dylan's frowning eyebrows and he does not hug her back. He stomps up the stairs, leaving a trail on the carpet behind him like a snail. Then the shower turns on. And a bit later, the door of Dylan's room clicks shut. Everyone sighs.

But Vincent gets up.

The
Purple Package

Vincent rummages in his backpack
and gets something
out. Before
he met Mum,
Vincent was a
backpacker who
travelled all
over the world.

He says his backpack was like his house, because it had everything he needed in it. He says that when you have to carry everything on your back all the time, you realize you don't actually need very much to survive, or even to be comfortable and happy. Even though he is not a backpacker any more, he says he will always keep his backpack, just to remind himself of that. It is one of the things he has been storing at Violet's house while they search for a new one.

Violet wonders if there is a tent in the backpack that Vincent is going to give Dylan to replace Dad's old leaky one. But even though tents can fold up to be quite small, the thing Vincent is getting out is much too small to be a tent. It is a dirty, flattish, purple cloth bag. Violet wonders what could be inside it. She knows it must be something important if it is one of the things Vincent carried on his back all over the world.

Vincent takes the bag upstairs and there is a little bit of knocking and some quiet talking and then the sound of Dylan's door clicking open. Mum and Violet and Nicola try to pretend they're not listening, but really they all are. They can't make out any words, but they can tell that there is no crossness in the talking.

★   ★   ★

In the morning the storm is finished
and there are voices in the garden.
Violet wakes up and looks out of
her window. Vincent is down there
with Dylan and they are dragging
everything out of the tent and putting
it out in the sun to dry. Dylan's
sleeping bag is hanging from the
branches of a tree. His pillow and his
pillowcase are laid out on the grass and
his violin case (which is waterproof,
luckily) and bits and pieces of his chess
set are strewn along the path.

While everything is drying in the
sun, Dylan and Vincent sit beside the
tent and Vincent opens the purple bag.

Violet watches closely through her
bedroom window. Inside the bag
is some red, stiffish material, some
needles, some green thread, a pair of
scissors and something that looks
a bit like a tube of toothpaste,
only smaller. Vincent cuts
two pieces of material about
the same size and Dylan squeezes
stuff from the tube onto them.
They put a piece on each side of a
hole in the tent and press hard. Then
they cut more pieces and stick them
over the other holes. Later on, when
the stuff from the tube has had time
to dry, they sew all round the patches
with the green thread and needles

and put more of the stuff in the tube on top of that.

By the time Violet has finished her breakfast, Dylan's tent is covered in red patches with green stitching. And by the time the patching is finished and the tent is back up again, most of Dylan's wet things are almost dry. Violet thinks the tent looks even better with the patches and stitching.

After that, Dylan decides to stay in his tent. Mum, Nicola, Vincent and Violet wish that he wanted to come back inside the house, but they are glad that at least the tent is not leaky any more.

All through the day, Violet admires the patchy tent. Later on, in the

night-time, when Violet wakes up,
wishing they could all stay for ever
in their house with the nice smell of
ginger cake and the small kitchen
spider, she tiptoes over to the window
and looks at the tent in the garden.
Dylan is awake too and is reading
with his torch, making the
patches glow like
stained glass.

The Wedding Preparations

It is the day before the wedding, and the Mackerels and Vincent are nearly ready.

Wedding ♡ checklist
1. Outfits ✓
2. Food ✓
3. Flowers ✓
4. Guests ✓

They have found a new house with enough rooms for everyone

and also room in the back garden for Dylan's tent if he would like to put it up again. Mum says there is enough space for the dining table and Vincent says it should stay coolish in the summer as long as everyone remembers to pull down the blinds. So now no one has to house-hunt any more, which Violet is glad about. But it does mean that they are really, definitely moving house, which is a thought that gives Violet's heart a slight squeezing feeling. But everyone except Dylan is busy organizing the last of the special things for the wedding, so there is not much extra time for worrying.

Vincent is finishing the wedding arch

and all there is left to do is to wind ivy around it and put white flowers on, which they will do in the morning just before the guests arrive, so that it will look nice and fresh. Violet thinks it would look even nicer if it did not have to go next to Dylan's tent. Mum says no one is going to make Dylan move it if he doesn't want to. Violet wonders if he would mind her decorating it with ivy and white flowers so it could at least match the arch.

Mum is adding the finishing touches to her wedding dress.

It is long and has a train and tiny pearls sewn on the front called seed pearls, which were from her mum's wedding dress.

Violet and Nicola are making sparkles for Mum's hair by gluing some of Nicola's sparkles onto hair slides. And they save some sparkles to glue onto Mum's white slippers so they will match too. When Mum tries it all on, Violet thinks she looks like a lady in a magazine. She and Nicola stare at her.

Mum looks at herself in the mirror
and twirls. Violet has never seen
Mum twirl before, or even look in
the mirror much, except
when she has
been hugging
someone who was
eating toast and
she is checking
to see if there
is Vegemite on
her. But this is
a different sort
of looking and
twirling. Mum
looks like a
princess.

At first Violet was bit disappointed that Mum wasn't going to have wings on her wedding dress, but then Mum had the good idea that Violet's dress could have wings if she liked. So they have sewn some onto one of Mum's nighties and trimmed it to the right length, and that is what Violet is 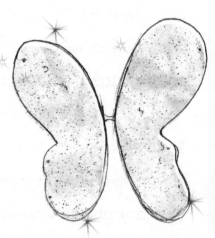 going to wear for the wedding.

Nicola is going to wear a party dress that got too short (after she got quite tall). Mum has helped her make some matching trousers that go under it.

Vincent is going to wear a waistcoat that Mum made for him. He says he might comb his hair but he is not making any promises. Violet has never seen Vincent with combed hair before because when you are a backpacker you don't bother much with combing. Mum says she doesn't really mind as long as there aren't any actual leaves or twigs in Vincent's hair, which there sometimes are when he has been out in the garden working on the wedding arch.

In the evening, when everything is as ready as it can be, Mum writes a letter to Dylan. She puts it in an envelope with a photo. Mum does not show Violet the letter because it is just

for Dylan, but
she does show
her the photo.
It is of
Mum, Dad,
Nicola and Dylan
camping in the tent when
it was new, before it got leaky and
musty. Mum is holding Nicola's hand
and Nicola is smaller than Violet is
now. Even though Dylan is quite a
small toddler, he is the tallest in the
photo because he is sitting up on Dad's
shoulders, smiling and waving.

"Where was I?" asks Violet.

"You hadn't been born yet," says
Mum.

It is funny seeing photos of your family before you were born, Violet thinks, but it is a nice photo, especially of Dylan.

Later on, when she is supposed to be in bed, Violet looks out into the garden from her window and sees Mum unzipping the door of Dylan's tent, just enough to post the letter inside.

The Early Morning

Violet wakes up
very, very early
on the morning
of the wedding.
She thinks about
her dress with
wings, which is
an exciting thought.

She also thinks about the new house, which is a worrying thought. Neither thought is very helpful for getting back to sleep. Violet gets up and tiptoes over to her window.

Dylan is sitting in the garden by his tent, looking up at the little bit of morning light starting to creep into the sky. Mum says that when people are in their **personal space** with the door shut, it means they want to be by themselves. But Dylan is outside, not inside. Violet puts on her dressing-gown and slippers and tiptoes downstairs.

"I woke up and I can't get back to sleep," says Violet, sitting down beside her brother, just in case he is in the mood for talking back.

"Me neither," says Dylan.

He doesn't seem to mind
Violet being there.

"How do you go to the
toilet when you live in a
tent?" asks Violet.

She has been wondering
that for quite a long time.

"You dig a hole if you're doing real
camping," says Dylan, "but usually I
just sneak inside when you're all busy
or out house-hunting."

Then they don't say anything for a
little while – just think and watch the
creeping light. Even though they are
not saying anything, Violet wonders if

they might be thinking about
the same sorts of things. She
is thinking mostly about all
the different things they
have done in the garden
together, like the time
Dylan made her a
teepee out of sticks and
the time he grew
mushrooms in a
special box and
Violet helped him
pick them when

they were big enough to have with
dinner. Violet wonders if, like her,
Dylan is wishing and wishing that it
could be their garden for ever.

"Dylan," says Violet. "Do you have any **small things** that are a bit special but that you don't really need?"

"Is this for one of your theories?" asks Dylan.

"Sort of," says Violet.

Dylan rolls his eyes, but then he goes inside the tent and rummages.

 He comes out with an extra pawn from his chess set and a spare key from his violin case.

"Are these OK?"

Violet nods. She puts the cream-coloured chess piece and the tiny silver key in her dressing-gown pocket and takes them over to the fennel plant where she once buried a dead pet ladybird in one of Nicola's special matchboxes. There is a **small part** of Violet there, and a **small part** of Nicola, and Violet would like there to be a **small part** of Dylan too. Dylan watches.

Violet scoops some earth away with her fingers. Then she buries the chess piece and the key and pats the earth smooth on top. The fennel patch looks just the same as it did before, but it is not.

"What's your **theory** this time?" asks Dylan.

"It's the **Theory of Leaving Small Things Behind**," says Violet. "When you leave something **small** behind, maybe a **small part** of you gets to stay too."

Dylan rolls his eyes again. But then he smiles — just a small smile — for the first time since they were at the beach house.

Violet and Dylan sit for a bit longer. The light has crept over most of the sky now and there are only a few stars left.

"I don't want to leave this house," says Violet. "Even if my **theory** is right and part of us does get to stay here."

"Me neither," says Dylan.

"But I do want to be where everyone else is, even if it's not this house."

"Me too," says Dylan.

After a while Dylan gets up and starts pulling up the tent pegs.

"What are you doing?" asks Violet.

"I think the garden might look nicer for the wedding without the tent," he says.

Violet helps Dylan to pack everything up and they carry it all upstairs to his room as quietly as they can. Then they go back outside and Dylan rakes up some leaves and Violet sweeps the path, and they both look a bit worriedly at the rectangle of brownish, yellowish dead grass which had been underneath the tent. Dylan has the good idea of covering it with the picnic rug. It doesn't look too bad, Violet thinks, because it has flowers on it and is quite garden-like.

"What are you two doing?" asks Nicola, coming out in her dressing-gown.

"Getting the garden ready," says Violet.

Nicola has a good idea too. She goes back up to her room and brings down some of her extra paper cranes. She threads them on long silver strings and Dylan hangs them from a tree in the garden.

Violet
sprinkles some
glitter on the
path for Mum
and Vincent to
walk down.

A bit later on,
Mum comes outside, yawning, with a
cup of tea in her hand. "What are you
all— Oh!" gasps Mum.

Mum looks around at the freshly
raked garden and sees the paper cranes
dangling on silver threads, the flowery
picnic rug where the tent was, and the

glittery path sparkling in the morning sun.

When Dylan walks over to her and gives her a hug, it almost looks as though Mum is sparkling too.

"Thank you," says Mum, hugging back and smiling and nearly crying a little bit.

The Beautiful Wedding

There are quite a few other things to
do before the wedding begins.
Everyone helps Mum bring
out the dining table to put
the food and drinks on.

Dylan and Violet bring out every
chair in the whole house, so that all
the guests will have somewhere to sit.
Nicola ties white ribbons around each
of the chairs so that they will sort of
match. When Vincent arrives they put
up the archway and decorate it with

leaves and flowers.

Then everyone
has to get dressed
in their wedding
clothes. Violet
puts on her new
dress with wings
and Nicola puts
on her dress with
matching trousers.

Vincent puts on his
waistcoat and combs
his hair and Dylan
puts on
the tie that
Mum bought
him to wear
last year when
he won a certificate
for violin-playing.
Mum puts on
her beautiful
dress. Nicola
puts Mum's hair
sparkles in and Violet
puts on her perfume.
It is all very exciting.

When the guests begin to arrive, Mum and Vincent stay upstairs so it will be a surprise when they all see Mum in her wedding dress and Vincent with his combed hair. Violet, Nicola and Dylan have to open the door and show everyone where the garden is and which chair is whose.

Nicola's guest is her best friend Lara.

Violet's guest is the old lady Iris MacDonald, whom she met when she was in hospital having her tonsils out. Iris MacDonald has a beautiful flower garden and she has made

Mum a bouquet with lilies and forget-me-nots. Mum has said it's not too late for Dylan to invite a guest too, so he has asked Tim from next door.

Mum's sister arrives wearing a big hat with flowers and carrying a huge platter of fruit and bread and special cheeses.

Then Vincent's best friend Buzz arrives with an coolbag full of drinks and ice. Violet has never seen a person with curlier hair or bigger feet than Buzz. And if you say "Hello, Buzz the Fuzz", he says "Hello, Violet the Pilot" and pretends to be an aeroplane and lets you fly him. Violet quite likes Buzz.

Then the celebrant, who's conducting the ceremony, arrives and it is time for the wedding to begin. All the guests go quiet and Violet feels a bit nervous. The old lady Iris MacDonald has brought Violet and Nicola each a basket of petals to throw. Everyone is waiting.

Finally, Mum and
Vincent come out of
the back door and
everyone claps and Violet
and Nicola throw the petals. Mum
and Vincent walk along the sparkly
path and under the special archway
holding hands, and someone whispers,
"Don't they look lovely?"

Violet listens to the celebrant doing lots of talking and Mum and Vincent sometimes saying "we will" and "I do". Sometimes the celebrant has to say things twice because her voice is softish and Vincent is a little bit deaf. Then Buzz gives Vincent the ring to put on Mum's finger.

"I now pronounce you husband and wife," says the celebrant.

Dylan quickly gets up from his chair and goes inside. Mum and Vincent look worriedly at each other.

Violet and Nicola look worriedly at each other too.

"Shall I go on?" asks the celebrant.

"Yes, please," says Mum.

"Well, then," says the celebrant, "you may now kiss."

Just then there is a loud bumping noise and everyone, including Mum and Vincent, turns around and looks up. Dylan is in Violet's room, opening the upstairs window as wide as he can. Violet wonders even more worriedly what he is doing.

But then suddenly the garden fills with a lovely sound. It is a tune called "Pachelbel's Canon" and Dylan is playing it on his violin. Mum and Vincent look up with the biggest smiles of all.

"You may now kiss," says the celebrant, laughing.

Mum and Vincent kiss while the music plays and everyone claps and Violet and Nicola throw the rest of their petals.

All afternoon, while everyone is chatting and eating and looking at their paper cranes and Violet the Pilot is flying Buzz the Fuzz like a plane, people keep saying it was a beautiful wedding.

Violet is quite sleepy from her early start, but she thinks it was a beautiful wedding too.

The New House

On the very last day in the house
Violet has lived in her whole life,
it hardly feels like her house at all.

Vincent and
Buzz have
been moving
furniture in
Buzz's truck,

driving it to the new house. Nearly all
of the smaller things have been packed
up in big cardboard boxes

to go in the truck
too. The pictures
have been taken off
the walls and the rugs
have been rolled up.

Mum is even painting over the special
place in the doorway where she used
to measure everyone on their birthday
and draw a line and write their name
and their new age next to it, so they
could see how much they had grown
since last year. She says the new people
in the house will probably prefer a
doorway without writing and lines.

Mum asks Violet if she would like to help to paint the doorway. Violet definitely would not. What she would like to do is sit on her bed and have a little cry, but her bed is in the truck. So she goes upstairs to where her bed used to be, in the room that will be her **personal space** for a few more hours. There is one box there. Inside are some of Violet's books and puzzles, a doll, some pencils and Violet's **Box of Small Things**, which is mostly full of beads, buttons and bits of ribbon that she has found and kept. Everything else has been taken down into the truck already. Violet sits next to the box.

violet's
room

86

She does not close the door because she would actually quite like someone to come in and sit with her, even though they would have to sit on the floor. But everyone is busy.

Violet can hear Mum and Nicola downstairs, talking about the new house. Nicola is quite excited because her new bedroom is going to be bigger than her old one and she has been wanting a bigger room for a long time. Mum is quite excited too because there is going to be a room for her knitting and her sewing things,

which have been in baskets and boxes and all over the dining table for too long, she says. Vincent is very excited because he is planning a vegetable patch in the new garden and he has already bought some seedlings and a book about compost.

Dylan has been packing the very last box of things in his room. He is just walking past Violet's room to take it downstairs when he sees her.

"Are you all right in there, Violet?" he asks.

"Yes," says Violet. But a big tear is trickling down the side of her nose. Dylan puts his box down and comes in and gives her a cuddle.

There was no furniture in his tent either, so he doesn't mind sitting on the floor.

"Our house is all empty and echoey," says Violet. "It doesn't even look like our house any more. It feels as if none of us have ever lived here."

"I know what you mean," says Dylan. All the tissues are packed away in boxes but he wipes Violet's big tear away with his sleeve. He doesn't say  anything but Violet thinks that just knowing someone else feels a bit the same as you do can be just as helpful sometimes.

After a while, Dylan says, "Want to see something?" Violet does, so Dylan takes her into his room.

He shows Violet a little space where the windowsill doesn't quite meet the wall.

"I was thinking about the **Theory of Leaving** Small **Things Behind**," he says. He has tucked a tiddlywink in there, from the tin Dad gave him when he was much younger.

"Now maybe a part of you will get to stay here for ever," says Violet.

"That's what I thought," says Dylan.

Just then Vincent calls up the stairs, "Come on, you two, we're loading the last boxes into the truck now."

"I'd better take our boxes down," says Dylan. "Will you be all right?"

"Yes," says Violet.

Before Dylan takes the last of Violet's things downstairs, she takes out her **Box of Small Things**.

"I'll need this just for a minute,' she says.

When Dylan has gone downstairs with the others and she is all by herself again, she pulls up the carpet in the corner of her room where it has always curled up a little bit. Underneath the carpet are wooden floorboards with thin little cracks between them. Violet pushes a small red button into one of the cracks and then smooths the carpet back down again. It looks exactly as it did a moment before.

Next Violet goes over to the other corner of the bedroom where the thick paint on the walls has peeled a little bit. Standing on her tiptoes, she tweaks a tiny gold sequin in behind the peel of paint. Nobody would ever guess it was there.

Finally, she goes over to the window and feels behind the curtains for the string you pull to make them open and close. She ties a small piece of purple ribbon around the string and pushes it up as high as she can.

It will probably never be noticed by anyone.

When she has finished, she closes her **Box of** small **Things** and gets ready to leave her room for the very last time. Everyone is calling her from downstairs and saying, "Hurry up, Violet!" and "Get a move on, please!" but she turns around for just one last look at her empty room.

Places, even **personal spaces**, look the same after Violet has been in them. But they are not.

Violet has to have her tonsils out.

And that's all right, because maybe Violet will make the most REMARKABLE RECOVERY ever.

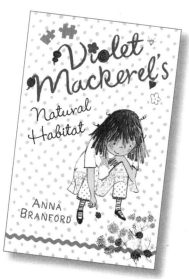

VIOLET MACKEREL quite likes helping.

But sometimes it's hard to know the best way to help a SMALL THING – especially when it's not in its NATURAL HABITAT.

ANNA BRANFORD was born on the Isle of Man, but spent her childhood in Sudan, Papua New Guinea and Australia. Once, when she was very itchy with the chicken pox, her dad read her *The Very Hungry Caterpillar* thirty times in a row.

Anna lectures in Sociology at Victoria University, Australia, and spends her evenings writing children's stories, kept company by a furry black cat called Florence. She also makes dolls using recycled fabric and materials.

SAM WILSON graduated from Kingston University in 1999 and has since been working on lots of grown-up books. The Violet Mackerel books are the first titles she has illustrated for children. She says, "I have always wanted to illustrate for children, it has been such fun drawing Violet, she is a gorgeous character with such an adventurous spirit." Sam lives in the countryside with her husband, two children, a black Lab called Jess and several chickens.